THE
AMERICAN WEI

by Marion Hess Pomeranc

illustrated by DyAnne DiSalvo-Ryan

Albert Whitman & Company
Morton Grove, Illinois

For Lona and Harry Hess and for Rita and Joseph Pomeranc...
immigrants, Americans. —M.H.P.

Wei to go!— Miss Sailboat and her readers. —D.D.-R.

Dent, ząb, jino, and *je-kuh-yah-chi* mean "tooth" in French, Polish, Kiswahili, and Chinese.
Hasta luego means "see you later" and *¿qué pasó?* means "what happened?" in Spanish;
s'il vous plaît means "if you please" and *voilà* means "there it is" in French.

Library of Congress Cataloging-in-Publication Data
Pomeranc, Marion Hess.
The American Wei / by Marion Hess Pomeranc ; illustrated by DyAnne DiSalvo-Ryan.
p. cm.
Summary: When Wei Fong loses his first tooth while going to his family's
naturalization ceremony many soon-to-be Americans join in the search.
ISBN 0-8075-0312-6
I. DiSalvo-Ryan, DyAnne, ill. II. Title
[1. Naturalization—Fiction. 2. Emigration and immigration—Fiction. 3. Chinese Americans—Fiction. 4. Tooth Fairy—Fiction.]
PZ7.P76955Am 1998 97-18202
[E]—dc21 CIP AC

The illustrations were rendered in gouache and pencil on 300-pound Lanaquarelle paper.
The text was set in FC Contemporary Brush.
Title calligraphy by Al Holter.
Designed by Scott Piehl.

About Naturalization

Every year, thousands of immigrants become new citizens of the United States in a process called *naturalization*. Though most Americans are automatically citizens by birth, our naturalized citizens were born in other countries and moved to the United States by choice.

Before they are naturalized, all citizens-to-be must meet many requirements. First, they have to receive permission to move to the United States permanently. Then they must live here for at least five years. After this time, they may apply for naturalization. If their application is approved, the next step is to take an examination. They must prove they can speak, read, and write English and show a knowledge of our history and government. For kids, it's easier. Children under eighteen become citizens along with their parents.

Soon after they pass the examination, the citizens-to-be are invited to a naturalization ceremony. This can take place in front of a judge or before an officer of the U.S. Immigration and Naturalization Service. At the ceremony, the applicants must take the Oath of Allegiance. Raising their right hands, they swear to give up any loyalty to a foreign country and to support and defend the Constitution and laws of the United States. Then they are citizens!

At many naturalization ceremonies, the new Americans pledge allegiance to the flag and sing the national anthem in celebration. For this is the day the naturalized citizens, like millions of immigrants before them, are given the same rights, privileges, and responsibilities as every other U.S. citizen (except that they may not become president or vice-president). The United States is now their home country.

That's the American Way.

Wei Fong popped up in front of the hand-carved mirror. The one that had come all the way from China—just as he had.

He touched his hair. He tugged at his suit.

"Hurry, we'll be late," he called.

Then he wiggled his tooth. It was very loose. He liked the way it felt as it rocked back and forth in his mouth.

Wei smiled. *Today might be a double-lucky day*, he thought. *In three hours, I'll be an American citizen. And maybe, just maybe, I'll lose my tooth today, too. Then the Tooth Fairy will visit me for the very first time.*

"I'm almost done," said Mama, poking her head out from the kitchen. "We'll have dim sum and hot dogs when we get back. I want everything just right."

"Hurry, Papa," Wei said, running into his parents' bedroom.

"...Jefferson, Madison, Monroe...," Papa was saying as he straightened his tie.

"Papa, you took your test months ago," Wei said. But he knew his father was proud that he remembered every president's name.

Finally, everyone was ready. The family dashed out
the door. They flew down four flights of stairs.
  "¡Hasta luego!" called Mrs. Ramos
from the landing.

"Good luck today," said Mr. Abramowitz
as he walked into the building.

"Mr. Abramowitz, could you take a picture of my
family?" Papa asked. "I promised to send Great-Uncle
Bing in China pictures of this day."

"Say 'pickled herring,' " said Mr. Abramowitz, snapping the
shutter. *Click*, and they were on their way.

"I think it's to the left," said Mama when they arrived downtown. She pointed toward a block filled with tall buildings and whizzing cars.

"I think it's over there," said Papa, pointing the other way.

"I know we'll be late now," said Wei, his tongue rocking the *very* wobbly tooth.

The family ran left. They ran right. They ran all around the block. They found it. The federal courthouse!

"One more picture," said Papa.

People hurried into the building. Many were there to become citizens that day, too.

"Where's Wei?" Mama suddenly asked, turning her head.

Mama and Papa dashed back to the street. Papa looked behind a pretzel vendor's cart.

Mama looked under a bench.

"He's dead!" cried Mama, running toward the curb.
Wei was on the ground. His nose was pointed down.
"My son!" cried Papa.
"My tooth!" cried Wei. "I lost it! Don't move!"

Mama and Papa joined Wei on the ground. They ran their hands over the sidewalk. Their fingers followed trails of long cracks.

No tooth.

"We have to go," said Papa.

"We'll miss the ceremony," said Mama.

Wei began to cry. "I need my tooth for the Tooth Fairy," he said.
Then Papa jumped up. "I found it!"
Wei's tears got bigger. His sobs got louder. "That's a pebble,"
he wailed.

"¿Qué pasó?" asked a woman with a cane.

"Our son lost his tooth," Papa explained.

The woman joined in the search.

"Step aside, s'il vous plaît," warned a stout man. He waved
Le Monde, his newspaper, to direct people around the
tooth-seekers.

Soon a family from Poland stopped to help. And a couple from
Kenya. And a tall man from Trinidad, too.

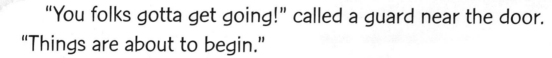

"You folks gotta get going!" called a guard near the door.
"Things are about to begin."

The search for the tooth sped up.

"Voilà!" said the stout man. "La dent!"

The woman with the cane triumphantly held out something in her hand.

"The tooth!" said the tall man from Trinidad.

"Ząb!" said the family from Poland.

"Jino!" said the couple from Kenya.

"這顆牙齒!" said Wei's parents. "Je-kuh-yah-chi!"

Wei wiped his eyes. "My tooth! Thank you," he said.

The new friends cheered as Mama wrapped Wei's tooth
in a tissue. Then everyone scrambled to the courthouse.
   They squished into an elevator and rode up eight floors.
Together, the group slipped through two big doors.

"Step up, don't be shy," said a man wearing a badge with a star. He was a federal marshal. "You'll all be sworn-in citizens soon."

Mama, Papa, and Wei slid down a long wooden bench.

"I've got a lot of people here," said the marshal to Mama. "Move down, ma'am. There's always room for one more."

With a quick wiggle, Mama got closer to the woman from Kenya.

Wei waited patiently as the grownups walked up to a clerk to sign their certificates of naturalization.

"I've got something for you," said Mama when she returned. She gave Wei a large white envelope. Inside was a letter from the president of the United States!

Then the room grew quiet.

"Hear ye, hear ye," said the clerk. "All rise."

A woman wearing a long black robe walked in and sat down at the front of the room.

"That's the judge," said Papa.

"Be seated," said the clerk.

"This is a special day. Welcome," said the judge.

"May I have my tooth?" whispered Wei to Mama.

Wei held his tooth carefully. It was so small! He listened as the judge talked about becoming an American citizen. He saw the marshal open the doors so friends and relatives could watch and listen, too.

Suddenly Mama poked Wei. "Stand up," she whispered. "It's time to take the Oath of Allegiance."

"I hereby declare on oath..." the people from many lands said together as they promised loyalty to their new nation. And when they were done, they were citizens of the United States!

Now the friends and relatives rose, too. They placed their hands over their hearts to join the new Americans in the Pledge of Allegiance. "...with liberty and justice for all," the voices rang out.

Then everyone sang "The Star-Spangled Banner."

Some people clapped. Others cried. Wei kissed Papa and
Mama. He felt a tear on Mama's cheek.

Wei opened the hand that had been over his heart. He smiled
at his tooth.

"One more picture, please," said Papa.

That afternoon, Wei's family and their friends feasted on
dim sum and hot dogs. Everything was just right.

When nighttime came, Wei stuck his letter from the president on his wall and slipped into bed. He carefully placed his tooth under his pillow.

"Will the Tooth Fairy know I'm an American citizen now?" he wondered as he fell asleep.

And she did.